The Hero's Journey For Modern Writers

Mike Martin

Mike Martin

Copyright © 2024 by Mike Martin

All rights reserved.

No portion of this book may be reproduced in any form without written permission from the publisher or author, except as permitted by U.K. copyright law.

Contents

1. How To Use This Resource — 1
2. Everyday Life — 6
3. The Opportunity — 10
4. Doubt & Hesitation — 15
5. Finding a Guide — 20
6. Going All In — 25
7. Challenges & Connections — 30
8. Facing The Big Test — 35
9. The Turning Point — 40
10. The Breakthrough — 45
11. The Journey Home — 50
12. The Final Challenge — 55
13. Back To Reality, Changed — 60

14.	Example Outline - Jack The Soldier	65
15.	Example Outline - Emily & Mark	74
16.	Example Outline - Max The Dog	83
17.	Example Outline - Emma & Ted	92
18.	Example Outline - Mike & Sarah (comedy)	102
19.	Example Outline - Mark & Emma	112
20.	Final Chapter: A Practical Tool for Writers	123
21.	More Books by Mike Martin	126

Chapter One

How To Use This Resource

This was never intended to be a book. It was created for my personal use, to make my storytelling process more efficient and structured. As someone who writes a lot of sales stories—and stories in general—I needed a system to structure them properly. One of my books, The Sales Parables, is filled with stories of people in sales, and through writing it, I realised the importance of structuring a story so that it pulls the reader in emotionally. I needed to build a connection with the reader, make them feel the pain of the challenge, and then see the hero triumph at the end.

To learn how to do this, I studied storytelling frameworks like Joseph Campbell's The Hero with a Thousand Faces, The Writer's Journey by Christopher Vogler, and Michael Hague's discussions on the Hero's Journey. All of these resources were insightful and fascinating, but what I really needed was something simpler. I didn't want to carry around a 300-page book just to reference a framework, so I decided to create my own condensed version—a pamphlet, essentially.

I started with Joseph Campbell's Hero's Journey and adapted it to my understanding, renaming some steps that didn't fully resonate with me. Terms like "The Innermost Cave" didn't quite click, so I simplified and restructured it in a way that made more sense to me. Here's the version I came up with, which breaks down into 12 steps:

1. Everyday Life
2. The Opportunity
3. Doubt and Hesitation
4. Finding a Guide
5. Going All In

6. Challenges and Connections

7. Facing the Big Test

8. The Turning Point

9. The Breakthrough

10. The Journey Home

11. The Final Challenge

12. Back to Reality, Changed

When I'm writing now, I don't need to keep referring to massive books. I write down these 12 headings, and under each, I fill in the relevant details for the story. It keeps me focused and ensures that I'm structuring my story properly without getting confused or bogged down.

To make this process even quicker, I've included summaries at the beginning and end of each chapter. After reading through the full chapter a couple of times, these summaries serve as quick refreshers, so you can glance at them and instantly recall what each step entails. This saves time and keeps you from having to re-read every chapter in detail.

This approach is designed for anyone who wants to outline their stories efficiently. Whether you're writing short stories, novels, or screenplays, these 12 steps are built on proven storytelling techniques and will help you structure your narrative without having to dive into lengthy books each time. It allows you to write faster and more effectively by focusing on the key elements of the story.

All you need to do is list the 12 steps, write brief descriptions for each, and you're ready to start. Of course, creating characters and developing your story's unique elements is still important, but this structure will make that process 10 times easier. Because I've kept this as short and simple as possible, you can quickly flip through it and know exactly how to proceed.

The goal is to give you a tool you can carry anywhere—whether in your laptop bag or alongside your writing pad—without the burden of carrying a large book. I prefer paperback over digital copies, so I keep this on me wherever I go. It's streamlined to eliminate unnecessary fluff and helps you jump straight into the writing process.

So, if you're like me and want a modern, easy-to-understand guide to writing structured stories, this will be incredibly helpful. Of course, I encourage you to read the full-length books I've mentioned for deeper learning, but this will be your go-to reference for fast, structured writing on the go.

All the best,

Mike Martin

https://mikemartin.uk

Chapter Two

Everyday Life

Summary: The hero's normal world before the adventure begins, where they're living an ordinary, relatable life.

Everyday Life is a crucial element in storytelling, particularly in narrative structures like Joseph Campbell's Hero's Journey. This is the phase before the protagonist embarks on their adventure, and it plays a vital role in grounding the story in a relatable context. In both fiction and real life, the depiction of everyday life allows the audience to connect with the hero, offering a glimpse into their world before the excitement and challenges of the story begin. This stage is important because it sets the foundation for the protagonist's eventual transformation, highlighting the contrast between who they are at the beginning of the journey and who they become by the end.

In many ways, everyday life represents stability, comfort, and predictability. The hero is typically shown living in a routine, whether it's mundane or somewhat fulfilling. This phase reflects the normalcy that most people experience in their own lives, which makes the character more relatable. Audiences get to see what the hero's world is like—what motivates them, what they care about, and what they believe. For example, in The Lion King, Simba's everyday life in the Pride Lands represents a carefree existence where he is safe, surrounded by loved ones, and unaware of the struggles that await him. This ordinary world contrasts starkly with the trials and challenges he will face later, which makes his journey more impactful.

Everyday life also serves to highlight the protagonist's strengths and weaknesses. It is in this familiar setting that their internal conflicts, desires, and frustrations are often revealed. For example, in The Matrix, Neo's ordinary life as a computer hacker and corporate employee reflects his feelings of dissatisfaction and his yearning for something more. He senses that there is a deeper truth to life, but he is trapped in a monotonous routine that holds him back. The depiction of this everyday life helps the audience understand Neo's inner conflict and desire for change, making it easier to root for him when the adventure begins.

In addition to building empathy and relatability, everyday life is important because it establishes what is at stake for the hero. By showing the hero's life before they embark on their journey, the audience can see what they stand to lose or leave behind. This makes the adventure more emotionally charged. For example, in The Hobbit, Bilbo Baggins' life in the Shire is peaceful, filled with the comforts of home, food, and routine. When he is called to leave this life behind for an uncertain and dangerous journey, the audience feels the weight of his decision because they have seen the comfort and stability he is giving up.

Another purpose of everyday life is to provide a clear starting point for the hero's transformation. By depicting the hero's normal world in detail, the story sets the stage for the hero's growth and change throughout the journey. The contrast between the ordinary and the extraordinary helps to highlight the significance of the hero's transformation. In many stories, the hero begins in a state of complacency or ignorance, unaware of the adventure or growth that awaits them. This transformation is more meaningful because it shows how far the hero has come by the end of the journey. The mundane routine of their previous life is replaced with wisdom, courage, or newfound purpose.

Everyday life serves as the backdrop for the hero's journey, providing a relatable and stable starting point that contrasts with the challenges and transformations to come. It helps the audience understand the hero's world, motivations, and what's at stake, while also providing a foundation for the protagonist's growth. This phase in storytelling is essential for building empathy, creating tension, and setting up the hero's eventual transformation, making the journey itself more compelling and meaningful.

Chapter Three

The Opportunity

Summary: The hero is presented with a new challenge, problem, or opportunity that shakes up their everyday routine and requires action.

The Opportunity, also known as the Call to Adventure in many storytelling structures, is the moment when the hero is presented with a chance to leave their familiar, everyday life and step into the unknown. This step marks the beginning of the hero's journey and is a key turning point in the narrative. It shakes up the status quo and offers the protagonist a path toward growth, change, and transformation. The Opportunity is more than just an invitation to adventure—it's the moment that defines the stakes of the story and sets the hero on a course they can't easily turn back from.

In most stories, the Opportunity appears as an external event or internal realisation that creates a sense of urgency or necessity for the hero. It could come in the form of a challenge, a discovery, or a personal crisis. For instance, in Star Wars: A New Hope, Luke Skywalker's opportunity arrives when he receives a message from Princess Leia via R2-D2. This message draws him into the galactic conflict and sets him on a path to leave his quiet farm life behind. The Opportunity doesn't always have to be dramatic; it can also be subtle, like a growing sense of dissatisfaction with life, as seen in The Matrix, when Neo's curiosity about the nature of reality leads him to discover the truth about the Matrix.

The Opportunity is significant because it disrupts the hero's ordinary world. The life they once knew is no longer sustainable or satisfying, and the chance to step into a new world—whether it's a physical journey or an internal one—becomes inevitable. This moment introduces the hero's choice: to remain in the comfort of the known or to embrace the uncertainty of the unknown. While many heroes initially hesitate, this opportunity often presents them with something they deeply need, even if they don't recognise it at first. This duality creates tension and sets up the internal conflict that the hero must wrestle with as they move forward.

In many narratives, the Opportunity also serves as a way to introduce the stakes of the story. What will happen if the hero seizes the opportunity, and what will happen if they don't? By clearly defining what's at risk, the story gives the audience a reason to invest in the hero's decision. In The Lord of the Rings, Frodo's opportunity comes when he learns about the true nature of the One Ring. The stakes are made clear: if the ring isn't destroyed, the entire world is at risk. This not only forces Frodo into action but also gives the audience a sense of the epic scale of the journey ahead.

Additionally, the Opportunity serves to test the hero's character. Their response to this moment often reveals much about who they are. Some heroes embrace the chance for adventure with enthusiasm, while others resist, overwhelmed by fear or doubt. In The Hunger Games, Katniss Everdeen seizes the opportunity when she volunteers to take her sister's place in the Games, showcasing her selflessness and courage. This not only sets the stage for her journey but also deepens the audience's connection to her character by revealing her motivations and values.

The Opportunity is also the doorway to the unknown. It represents the threshold the hero must cross to enter a world that is different from what they've known. This new world might be a literal new environment, like Dorothy being swept away to Oz in The Wizard of Oz, or a figurative one, like a shift in perception or responsibility. Either way, the Opportunity signifies the end of the hero's ordinary life and the beginning of something extraordinary.

The Opportunity is a critical step in storytelling, acting as the catalyst that launches the hero into their journey. It creates the tension between the familiar and the unknown, introduces the stakes, and tests the hero's willingness to change. Without this moment, the hero would remain stuck in their ordinary world, and the story would never truly begin. The Opportunity is the gateway to adventure, transformation, and the challenges that will ultimately define the hero's growth and the story's outcome.

Chapter Four

Doubt & Hesitation

Summary: The hero resists stepping into the unknown because of fear, uncertainty, or discomfort with change.

Doubt and hesitation are crucial elements in the hero's journey, often referred to as the Refusal of the Call in Joseph Campbell's Hero's Journey or Christopher Vogler's Writer's Journey. These moments of uncertainty occur right after the hero is presented with the opportunity for change or adventure, but before they fully commit to it. This stage is vital for creating tension and emotional complexity, as it shows the hero's vulnerability and humanity. They are not invincible or fearless; instead, they experience real-world doubts that make them more relatable and realistic to the audience.

At its core, doubt and hesitation reflect the hero's internal struggle. Faced with the unknown, the hero is likely to question their abilities, the potential risks, and the wisdom of leaving behind the comfort of their familiar world. This hesitation is a natural response to fear of change, uncertainty, or danger. It often manifests as a moment of introspection, where the hero asks themselves whether they are ready or capable of embarking on the journey ahead. This doubt makes the hero's decision to ultimately move forward more powerful because it shows that they had to overcome significant internal barriers.

In many stories, the doubt and hesitation phase helps the audience connect with the hero on a deeper level. By seeing the hero struggle with self-doubt, the audience recognises the hero's humanity and their fear of failure, which are feelings most people experience in real life. These moments of hesitation make the hero's eventual success or growth more meaningful because they demonstrate that the hero is not infallible. Instead, they must muster the courage to overcome their fears. This emotional complexity elevates the hero's journey, making it not just about external challenges, but about internal transformation as well.

One famous example of doubt and hesitation can be found in The Matrix, when Neo is offered the choice between the red pill and the blue pill by Morpheus. Neo hesitates before making his decision. He is torn between the safety of his familiar but false reality and the terrifying unknown of the truth. His doubt highlights the weight of the decision he must make, as accepting the call to adventure will forever change his life. This internal conflict adds depth to Neo's character and makes the moment when he finally accepts the red pill all the more significant.

Doubt and hesitation also serve to raise the stakes of the story. The hero's reluctance often underscores the dangers or sacrifices that lie ahead. Whether it's the fear of physical danger, the emotional toll of leaving loved ones behind, or the anxiety of stepping into a role they may not feel ready for, this hesitation reminds the audience of the high cost of the journey. It adds weight to the decision and allows the audience to feel the hero's conflict, heightening the tension before the adventure truly begins.

Additionally, this phase in the story may also allow other characters to play a crucial role in nudging the hero forward. A mentor or guide often steps in at this point, helping the hero navigate their doubts. For example, in The Hobbit, Gandalf persuades Bilbo Baggins to join the adventure, despite Bilbo's hesitation. The intervention of a mentor can give the hero the push they need to confront their doubts and take the first step toward transformation. In many stories, this is where the mentor offers wisdom, guidance, or reassurance, showing the hero that the risks of the journey are worth the rewards.

Finally, doubt and hesitation serve to make the hero's journey more rewarding for the audience. Without hesitation, the hero's success could feel too easy or inevitable. By showing that the hero struggles with fear or uncertainty, the story creates a sense of risk and challenge. The audience becomes more invested in the hero's growth because they have seen the obstacles—both external and internal—that the hero must overcome.

Doubt and hesitation are essential parts of the hero's journey, adding emotional complexity, raising the stakes, and making the hero's eventual commitment to the journey more impactful. This phase reminds us that even the greatest heroes experience fear and uncertainty, making their journey toward transformation all the more powerful and relatable.

Chapter Five

Finding a Guide

Summary: The hero meets a mentor, coach, or inner wisdom that gives them the tools, knowledge, or encouragement they need to move forward.

Finding a Guide is a pivotal moment in storytelling, particularly in narrative structures like the Hero's Journey. This step occurs when the hero, grappling with doubt and uncertainty about embarking on their adventure, encounters a mentor or guide who provides the knowledge, tools, or encouragement necessary for the journey ahead. The guide can take many forms—sometimes it's a wise mentor, a supportive friend, or even an internal realisation. Regardless of form, the guide plays a crucial role in helping the hero take the next step toward growth and transformation.

At its core, finding a guide represents the moment when the hero receives crucial support. This mentor figure often embodies wisdom and experience, offering the hero insight into the journey ahead and helping them overcome the fear or uncertainty that has been holding them back. In stories, this guide is often someone who has already experienced their own version of the journey, giving them the authority to help the hero navigate the unknown. For example, in Star Wars: A New Hope, Obi-Wan Kenobi serves as Luke Skywalker's guide, introducing him to the ways of the Force and preparing him for the adventure ahead. Obi-Wan's wisdom and knowledge of the Force give Luke the confidence and tools he needs to step into his destiny.

In many stories, the guide doesn't just provide practical tools but also acts as a moral or philosophical compass for the hero. They help the hero see the larger purpose of their journey and understand the consequences of their choices. This is especially true in narratives where the hero is struggling with internal conflicts or doubts about their own abilities. The guide helps the hero see their own potential and the importance of the journey, reinforcing the value of leaving behind the safety of the ordinary world. In The Matrix, Morpheus serves as Neo's guide, offering him not just the physical training he needs to fight in the Matrix, but also philosophical insight into the nature of reality and Neo's role in the rebellion against the machines. Morpheus helps Neo understand that the journey is not just about survival, but about embracing a larger purpose.

The role of the guide also serves a symbolic function. Often, the guide represents the wisdom the hero needs to access within themselves. In some stories, the guide might be an actual person, like Dumbledore in Harry Potter, but in others, the guide could be a more abstract presence, such as an inner voice, an experience, or even a deep realisation about oneself. Regardless of form, the guide represents the external or internal force that helps the hero see what they are truly capable of. For example, in The Lion King, Simba finds his guide in Rafiki, the wise baboon who helps Simba reconnect with his past and his true identity. Rafiki acts as a catalyst for Simba's realisation that he must return to the Pride Lands and claim his rightful place as king.

Additionally, finding a guide helps raise the stakes of the story. It signals to the audience that the journey is serious and requires preparation. The presence of a guide indicates that the hero cannot undertake the journey alone and that the challenges ahead are significant. The guide is there to equip the hero with the necessary tools, skills, or wisdom, making it clear that success on the journey will require more than just courage—it will require growth and learning.

However, it's important to note that the guide doesn't solve the hero's problems for them. While the guide provides essential support, the hero must still face their own challenges and make their own decisions. The guide's role is to empower the hero, not to lead the journey. In this way, finding a guide is less about dependency and more about the hero learning to stand on their own. For instance, in The Hunger Games, Haymitch serves as Katniss Everdeen's mentor, offering advice and strategies, but ultimately, Katniss must navigate the arena and make her own choices.

Finding a guide is a crucial moment in the hero's journey that provides the hero with the support and wisdom they need to face the challenges ahead. Whether in the form of a wise mentor, a symbolic figure, or an inner realisation, the guide helps the hero overcome their doubts and prepares them for the transformative journey. This relationship adds depth to the story, illustrating that no hero can succeed alone and that growth often requires learning from those who have gone before.

Chapter Six

Going All In

Summary: The hero commits to the adventure, leaving behind their comfort zone and stepping into a new, unfamiliar world filled with challenges.

Going All In is one of the most significant moments in the hero's journey. It represents the hero's commitment to the adventure, where they make the decisive choice to leave behind the comfort of the ordinary world and step into the unknown. This moment is often charged with emotion, as it marks a point of no return for the hero. Once they've gone all in, they cannot go back to the life they once knew, and they must now face the challenges and opportunities that come with the journey ahead.

This step is often a direct response to the Call to Adventure and follows the phase of Doubt and Hesitation, where the hero wrestles with their fears and uncertainties about stepping into the unknown. In Going All In, the hero makes a conscious decision to embrace the risks and challenges, knowing that this choice will forever change their life. This commitment signals the hero's growth as they begin to take control of their own destiny. For example, in The Matrix, Neo's decision to take the red pill is a perfect representation of this moment. By taking the red pill, Neo willingly abandons the false reality he's known his whole life, opting instead to explore a dangerous, unfamiliar world in pursuit of the truth. This leap is irreversible—once he takes it, there's no turning back.

Emotionally, Going All In represents a critical turning point for the hero. It is a moment where they must confront their fears head-on and trust in themselves, or in their guide, that they are capable of handling what comes next. This step highlights the courage and vulnerability of the hero, making their journey more meaningful. By committing to the adventure, the hero demonstrates that they are willing to face their fears in pursuit of something greater. In Harry Potter and the Philosopher's Stone, Harry's decision to board the Hogwarts Express and leave behind the abusive world of the Dursleys symbolises this leap into a new, magical world where he will face challenges, but also discover his true potential.

Going All In also raises the stakes in the story. Once the hero makes this commitment, they are now fully engaged in the journey, and the consequences of their decisions will have a more profound impact. The hero may not fully understand the magnitude of what they are stepping into, but they know that life as they knew it is no longer an option. In The Lord of the Rings, when Frodo decides to take the Ring to Mount Doom, he is committing to a dangerous and uncertain path. His leap into this responsibility transforms him from a simple hobbit into the bearer of a monumental burden, and the weight of that choice drives the rest of the narrative.

Symbolically, Going All In can represent a broader theme of personal transformation. It often coincides with the moment when the hero begins to shed their old self and embrace the potential of who they could become. The leap marks the hero's first active step toward becoming the person they are meant to be. In Mulan, the moment Mulan decides to disguise herself as a soldier and take her father's place in the army is her leap into a world of danger, but also one of self-discovery. She leaves behind her role as a dutiful daughter in a traditional household and steps into a journey that will allow her to prove her worth and find her true identity.

While Going All In can be daunting, it is a necessary part of the hero's growth. Without this moment of commitment, the hero would remain stuck in their ordinary world, never evolving or realising their full potential. It is the leap that begins the process of transformation, pushing the hero into the heart of the story's adventure.

Going All In is a crucial moment in the hero's journey, marking the hero's decision to fully embrace the adventure. It signifies courage, the acceptance of risk, and the beginning of the hero's transformation. By

Going All In, the hero commits to the unknown, setting the stage for the challenges, growth, and ultimate rewards that lie ahead. This moment is often what defines the hero's journey, as it represents the shift from passivity to action, from doubt to determination.

Chapter Seven

Challenges & Connections

Summary: The hero faces a series of tests and obstacles while forming alliances with others and encountering enemies or opposition.

Challenges and Connections is a key phase in the hero's journey, occurring after the hero has committed to their adventure by Going All In. This stage is crucial for the hero's development, as it forces them to confront obstacles that test their strength, resilience, and character. Simultaneously, the hero begins to form important relationships with allies, mentors, and even enemies, all of whom shape their journey. The combination of facing trials and building connections serves as the backbone of the hero's transformation, preparing them for the greater challenges that lie ahead.

At this point in the story, the hero has stepped into an unfamiliar world, whether physical or emotional, where the rules are different from what they've known. The challenges the hero faces in this stage are designed to push them outside their comfort zone and reveal areas where they need to grow. These tests are not always physical; they may be mental, emotional, or spiritual, presenting the hero with internal conflicts that force them to question their values, abilities, and purpose. For instance, in Harry Potter and the Sorcerer's Stone, Harry faces a series of challenges at Hogwarts, from navigating friendships and school life to uncovering the mystery of the Sorcerer's Stone. Each of these challenges not only tests his skills but also builds his confidence and shapes his character.

Challenges are essential for the hero's development because they provide opportunities for growth. By facing and overcoming obstacles, the hero gains new skills, knowledge, and self-awareness. These trials often come in increasing difficulty, preparing the hero for the ultimate test later in the story. They serve as a training ground, where the hero learns to apply the lessons they've gathered along the way. For example, in The Hunger Games, Katniss Everdeen faces a series of life-threatening challenges in the arena, each one forcing her to rely on her intelligence, survival skills, and instinct. These challenges not only test her physical abilities but also her moral compass, as she grapples with the consequences of taking lives to survive.

Alongside the challenges, connections are an equally important aspect of this stage. As the hero navigates this unfamiliar world, they form relationships with allies who offer support, guidance, or companionship. These connections can come in many forms—mentors who provide wisdom, peers who share the journey, or friends who offer emotional support. The bonds formed in this phase often become pivotal to the hero's success, as no hero can complete their journey alone. In The Lord of the Rings, Frodo forms strong connections with his fellow travellers, including Samwise Gamgee, who becomes his loyal companion. These relationships help Frodo endure the challenges ahead, giving him strength when he feels weak and reminding him that he is not alone in his quest.

However, the hero may also encounter enemies or antagonists during this phase, which adds complexity to the story. These antagonists can take the form of literal enemies who oppose the hero's goals or more symbolic representations of the hero's inner demons, fears, or doubts. The conflicts with these antagonists often deepen the hero's understanding of their own weaknesses and force them to confront the darker aspects of themselves. For example, in Star Wars: A New Hope, Luke Skywalker's encounter with Darth Vader represents not only a physical challenge but also an internal one, as Luke must come to terms with his own potential for darkness.

The relationships the hero builds in this phase also provide a sense of belonging and purpose. The hero often begins the journey feeling isolated, but through connections with others, they realise they are part of something bigger. This sense of community can be a powerful motivator for the hero, giving them the strength to continue despite the difficulties they face. In Mulan, Mulan initially struggles to fit in with her fellow soldiers, but as she proves her worth through shared challenges, she gains their respect and forms strong bonds of friendship that help her succeed.

Challenges and Connections is a critical stage of the hero's journey that combines personal trials with the formation of meaningful relationships. The challenges the hero faces push them to grow and prepare them for greater obstacles, while the connections they make offer essential support and guidance. Together, these elements form the foundation of the hero's transformation, shaping them into the person they need to become to face the ultimate test. This phase underscores the idea that growth often comes through struggle and that success is often a result of collaboration and connection with others.

Chapter Eight

Facing The Big Test

Summary: The hero prepares to confront their biggest challenge, whether it's an external threat or an inner struggle they need to overcome.

Facing the Big Test is a climactic moment in the hero's journey, representing the ultimate challenge that the hero has been preparing for throughout their adventure. This stage, often referred to as the Ordeal in Joseph Campbell's Hero's Journey, is the point at which the hero confronts their deepest fears, greatest obstacles, or most formidable enemies. It's a pivotal moment in the narrative, where everything the hero has learned and experienced is put to the test. Success or failure in this test can determine not only the hero's fate but also the outcome of the entire story.

At its core, Facing the Big Test is about transformation. This challenge is typically more than just a physical battle or a task to be completed. It is an emotional or psychological trial that forces the hero to confront their own inner demons, fears, or weaknesses. The hero must draw upon everything they have learned from previous trials, the guidance of mentors, and the strength they've gained from connections with allies. This test is not just about defeating an external enemy but often about conquering the hero's own limitations. In The Lord of the Rings, Frodo's big test is not just reaching Mount Doom, but also resisting the overwhelming temptation of the One Ring, which requires him to summon all his inner strength.

The stakes during the Big Test are usually at their highest. This moment often involves life-or-death decisions, not only for the hero but for others as well. It is the culmination of all the conflicts, challenges, and tension that have been building up throughout the story. The hero's actions in this moment will determine whether they succeed or fail in their mission. For example, in Harry Potter and the Philosopher's Stone, Harry's big test occurs when he confronts Professor Quirrell and Voldemort in the final act. The stakes are immense—Harry is fighting not only for his life but also to prevent Voldemort's return to power.

One of the key aspects of Facing the Big Test is the element of sacrifice. In many stories, the hero must give up something important to them, whether it's their personal safety, a cherished relationship, or even their life, in order to achieve victory. This sacrifice demonstrates the hero's growth and their commitment to the greater good. It's a moment where the hero proves their worth, showing that they are willing to go beyond their own interests for the sake of others. In The Hunger Games, Katniss faces her big test when she and Peeta are the last two tributes left. Instead of letting the Capitol force one of them to kill the other, she offers to take her own life, making a bold statement of defiance and sacrifice.

Facing the Big Test is also where the hero's transformation becomes most visible. The hero is no longer the person they were at the beginning of the journey. They have evolved through their experiences, challenges, and relationships. The test they face now reflects their growth. The hero is often called to make a difficult choice, one that tests not just their physical strength or intelligence but also their moral character. In Spider-Man, Peter Parker's big test comes when he must choose between saving Mary Jane and a group of innocent civilians. This moment forces him to embody the responsibility he's been grappling with throughout the story.

Additionally, Facing the Big Test provides an opportunity for the audience to witness the hero's full potential. All the skills, knowledge, and inner growth the hero has acquired are put to the ultimate test. The outcome of this challenge often defines the hero's legacy and cements their status as a true hero in the eyes of others. In The Matrix, Neo's big test occurs when he faces Agent Smith. This moment solidifies Neo's identity as "The One," as he fully embraces his power and role as the saviour of humanity.

Facing the Big Test is the most critical moment in the hero's journey. It is where the hero's growth is fully realised, and they are tested in ways that challenge not only their abilities but their very character. This climactic challenge carries the highest stakes and often involves sacrifice, transformation, and a moment of truth for the hero. Success in this test brings the hero to a new level of understanding, power, or wisdom, marking the culmination of their journey and preparing them for the final resolution of the story.

Chapter Nine

The Turning Point

Summary: The hero confronts their greatest fear or biggest challenge head-on, experiencing a critical moment of transformation.

The Turning Point is a critical moment in any narrative structure, signalling a profound shift in the story's direction and in the hero's journey. Often, this moment marks the hero's realisation or decision that changes the course of the plot, moving the story toward its climax and eventual resolution. It is at this juncture that the hero, having faced numerous challenges and internal conflicts, must make a key choice or confront a truth that alters their trajectory. This shift is not only pivotal for the plot but also for the hero's personal development, symbolising growth, enlightenment, or commitment to a new path.

In the hero's journey, the Turning Point often follows a period of trial and self-doubt. Up to this moment, the hero has faced smaller obstacles that test their abilities and beliefs. However, these challenges have been building toward a larger realisation or choice that will fundamentally change how the hero views themselves and their mission. This change is often emotional or psychological, representing a shift in the hero's mindset or understanding of their role. For example, in The Matrix, Neo's turning point occurs when he finally accepts that he is "The One," fully embracing his identity and power. This moment is a shift from doubt to certainty, changing not only his own fate but also the fate of the rebellion.

The Turning Point is also a moment of increased stakes. In many stories, this is the point where the hero realises the full scale of the conflict and what's truly at risk. This realisation compels them to commit more fully to their journey, knowing that the outcome of their choices will have far-reaching consequences. In

The Lion King, Simba's turning point comes when he speaks with the ghost of his father, Mufasa, and understands that he must return to the Pride Lands to reclaim his rightful place as king. The stakes are now higher than ever, as Simba recognises that his failure to act could mean the permanent downfall of his home.

This moment often involves a confrontation with a core fear or truth. The hero may have been avoiding this truth for most of the story, but the Turning Point forces them to face it head-on. This confrontation usually brings clarity and pushes the hero to make a decisive action. In Star Wars: The Empire Strikes Back, Luke Skywalker's turning point comes when he learns that Darth Vader is his father. This revelation shatters Luke's previous understanding of the conflict and forces him to confront the dark potential within himself. It is a moment of deep emotional turmoil, but it also serves as a catalyst for Luke's growth as he moves toward accepting his destiny.

Additionally, the Turning Point often involves a decision. This decision is usually a defining one that will set the hero on the final path toward the climax of the story. The choice the hero makes at this point reflects their growth and transformation. They are no longer the same person who started the journey—they are now equipped with the wisdom, strength, or courage needed to take on the final challenges. In The Hunger Games: Catching Fire, Katniss Everdeen's turning point comes when she decides to break free from the Capitol's control by joining the rebellion. This decision alters her role in the story from a survivor to a leader and symbol of revolution.

In some cases, the Turning Point also serves as a moment of alignment between the hero's internal and external struggles. Often, the hero's journey involves two layers of conflict: the external challenges posed by the antagonist or environment, and the internal conflicts within the hero's mind. At the Turning Point, these two elements often intersect. The hero's internal growth allows them to confront and resolve the external challenges in new, more effective ways. This alignment propels the story toward its climax, where both internal and external conflicts are resolved.

The Turning Point is a crucial narrative moment that marks a significant change in the hero's journey. It signals a moment of realisation, decision, or transformation that alters the course of the story and the hero's fate. This shift sets the stage for the story's climax, raising the stakes and deepening the emotional impact of the narrative. By confronting fears, making critical decisions, and embracing their true path, the hero steps into a new phase of their journey, preparing them for the final trials and the ultimate resolution of the story.

Chapter Ten

The Breakthrough

Summary: After overcoming the turning point, the hero gains a reward—whether it's knowledge, personal growth, or a tangible prize.

The Breakthrough is a pivotal moment in the hero's journey, where everything the protagonist has worked toward suddenly comes into focus. It is often the point where the hero experiences a profound realisation, gains a new level of understanding, or makes a crucial discovery that shifts the course of the story. The breakthrough can take many forms—internal clarity, a solution to a seemingly insurmountable problem, or the acquisition of a new skill or knowledge—but it always signifies a turning point that empowers the hero to push forward toward the final goal. It is the moment when the hero connects all the lessons and experiences from their journey, leading to a significant transformation.

In many stories, the Breakthrough is the culmination of the hero's internal struggles and external challenges. Up to this point, the hero has faced numerous tests that have forced them to grow, adapt, and confront their weaknesses. The breakthrough represents the moment when the hero moves beyond self-doubt, fear, or confusion and gains the confidence or insight needed to overcome their obstacles. In The Matrix, Neo's breakthrough occurs when he finally believes in his ability to manipulate the Matrix and becomes "The One." This realisation not only shifts his perception of reality but also allows him to defeat his enemies and take control of his destiny.

The Breakthrough often follows a period of intense difficulty or conflict, where the hero feels as though they are on the verge of failure. It is in this moment of darkness that the hero often finds the clarity or strength they need to succeed. This can be seen in The Lord of the Rings, where Frodo's breakthrough happens at the very end of his journey to destroy the One Ring. Despite his near-collapse from the weight of his mission, he is able to complete the task, largely due to the support of his friends and his newfound inner strength. The breakthrough, in this case, is not just about completing the mission but also about Frodo's emotional and spiritual transformation.

In many narratives, the Breakthrough involves a new understanding of the self. The hero often realises that the answers they have been seeking externally were within them all along. This internal epiphany often leads to the hero recognising their own power, resilience, or worth. For instance, in Mulan, Mulan's breakthrough comes when she accepts her true identity and stops trying to fit into the mould of a traditional soldier or daughter. This realisation allows her to fight with her unique strengths, ultimately leading to her victory against the Huns.

In some stories, the Breakthrough is tied to a specific event or revelation. The hero might discover a hidden truth or uncover an important piece of information that shifts the narrative. This breakthrough often brings new opportunities or paths that were previously closed off. In mystery or detective stories, the breakthrough might come when the protagonist finally pieces together the clues to solve the case. In Sherlock Holmes, for example, Holmes's breakthroughs often occur when he makes a key observation or deduction that leads him to the solution of the mystery. These moments of revelation give the hero the final piece of the puzzle needed to achieve success.

Another important aspect of the Breakthrough is its impact on the story's emotional arc. This moment is often deeply satisfying for the audience because it resolves tension that has been building throughout the narrative. The breakthrough validates the hero's struggles and sacrifices, showing that their perseverance has paid off. It also creates momentum, propelling the story toward its climax as the hero is now equipped with the knowledge, strength, or resources necessary to face the final challenge. In The Hunger Games, Katniss's breakthrough comes when she realises how to manipulate the rules of the Games to save both herself and Peeta. This realisation not only saves her life but also sets the stage for her eventual rebellion against the Capitol.

The Breakthrough is a key moment in the hero's journey, symbolising a shift in understanding, power, or capability that enables the hero to move forward with new confidence and purpose. Whether it is an internal epiphany, the discovery of vital information, or the resolution of a long-standing conflict, the breakthrough is the moment when everything changes for the hero. It transforms both the protagonist and the story, setting the stage for the final confrontation and ultimately leading to the hero's victory or resolution.

Chapter Eleven

The Journey Home

Summary: The hero starts their return to normal life, often facing new challenges or consequences from their previous actions.

The Journey Home is a crucial stage in the hero's journey, representing the hero's return to the ordinary world after achieving their goal or completing their quest. This phase is more than just a physical return; it symbolises the culmination of the hero's transformation, as they re-enter their familiar environment as a changed person. After having faced trials, experienced growth, and often made sacrifices, the hero must now reintegrate into the world they left behind. The Journey Home is often fraught with challenges of its own, as the hero must reconcile who they've become with the world that may not have changed in their absence.

In many stories, the Journey Home is a time of reflection for the hero. Having undergone a transformation, the hero now carries with them the knowledge, experience, and wisdom gained from their adventure. This phase allows them to process these changes and often involves a realisation of how much they have evolved. For instance, in The Lord of the Rings, Frodo returns to the Shire after destroying the One Ring, but he finds that he can no longer live the simple life of a hobbit. His experiences have changed him so profoundly that he feels disconnected from the world he once knew. The Journey Home thus becomes a moment where the hero understands that they cannot return to exactly who they were before, reflecting the often bittersweet nature of this phase.

The Journey Home can also be a time of external challenges. The hero's return is not always smooth, and they may encounter new obstacles as they try to integrate back into their former life. Sometimes, these challenges are a result of the unresolved consequences of their quest. For example, in The Odyssey, Odysseus's journey home is long and perilous, filled with dangers and delays that test his resilience even after he has completed his primary goal of defeating the Trojans. His journey home becomes an adventure in itself, demonstrating that the hero's trials are not necessarily over once the central quest is completed.

Additionally, the Journey Home often involves sharing the hero's newfound knowledge or gifts with their community. This concept is sometimes referred to as "returning with the elixir," where the hero brings back something valuable—whether it's wisdom, power, or literal treasure—that can benefit others. In many myths and stories, the hero's journey is not just about personal growth but also about contributing to the greater good. In The Lion King, for example, Simba returns to Pride Rock not only to reclaim his rightful place as king but also to restore balance and prosperity to the land that has suffered under Scar's rule. His return is a gift to his people, symbolising the completion of his transformation from a lost exile to a responsible leader.

The Journey Home is also a test of how well the hero can apply the lessons they've learned. In some cases, the hero is faced with a final challenge or temptation that tests their newfound strength or wisdom. This is often referred to as the "resurrection" phase of the hero's journey, where the hero faces one last ordeal before they can fully integrate into their old life. In Harry Potter and the Deathly Hallows, Harry's final journey home includes his confrontation with Voldemort. Though he has faced numerous trials before, this last battle is the ultimate test of his growth as a wizard and leader.

In many modern stories, the Journey Home also explores the theme of belonging. After undergoing significant changes, the hero may struggle with finding their place in the world they left behind. This tension between the old world and the new self can lead to feelings of alienation or restlessness. The hero may realise that they have outgrown their previous life, or that their new understanding of the world makes it impossible to return to who they once were. In The Hobbit, Bilbo Baggins returns to the Shire after his adventures, but he is no longer the same hobbit who left. While his fellow hobbits continue with their lives, Bilbo feels a sense of isolation, as his experiences have set him apart from the community he once belonged to.

The Journey Home is a vital phase of the hero's journey that reflects both the physical return to the ordinary world and the internal process of integrating the lessons learned. It is a time for the hero to reconcile their transformed self with the world they left behind, often facing new challenges and sharing the fruits of their adventure with others. This stage highlights the hero's growth and provides closure to the story, illustrating that even after the quest is completed, the hero's journey continues in new and profound ways.

Chapter Twelve

The Final Challenge

Summary: The hero faces a final test, where they prove how much they've changed. This is usually the climax of the story.

The Final Challenge is the climax of the hero's journey, the moment that brings together all the hero's skills, growth, and experiences into one decisive test. This stage, often referred to as the "Resurrection" or "Ultimate Ordeal" in storytelling structures like Joseph Campbell's Hero's Journey, represents the culmination of the hero's entire journey. It is the last and greatest obstacle that stands between the hero and the completion of their quest, and it often carries the highest stakes, both for the hero and for those they seek to protect. The Final Challenge is more than just a physical confrontation; it is often symbolic of the internal transformation the hero has undergone throughout their journey.

At its core, the Final Challenge forces the hero to confront the central conflict of the story. This conflict may be an external enemy, such as a villain or antagonist, or it could be an internal struggle, such as the hero's fears, doubts, or insecurities. In many cases, the hero's internal and external challenges are deeply intertwined, and the Final Challenge becomes a test of both physical ability and emotional strength. For example, in The Lord of the Rings: The Return of the King, Frodo's final challenge is not just the physical task of reaching Mount Doom and destroying the One Ring, but also the internal battle against the overwhelming temptation of the Ring's power. His struggle highlights the theme of inner strength and moral resilience, as the true victory is not just in destroying the Ring but in overcoming the seduction of evil.

The Final Challenge often carries life-or-death stakes, either for the hero, their loved ones, or even the larger world. This sense of urgency heightens the drama of the moment and emphasises the hero's growth and transformation. Everything the hero has learned throughout their journey comes to a head in this moment, and their actions here determine the outcome of the entire story. In Harry Potter and the Deathly Hallows, Harry's final challenge is his confrontation with Voldemort. It is not just about defeating a powerful enemy, but also about Harry's willingness to sacrifice himself for the greater good, symbolising his ultimate acceptance of responsibility and his understanding of the importance of love and selflessness.

The Final Challenge also represents the hero's full embrace of their identity and purpose. Up until this point, the hero may have struggled with self-doubt, uncertainty, or reluctance to fully step into their role. The Final Challenge forces them to confront and resolve these issues once and for all. In The Matrix, Neo's final confrontation with Agent Smith is not just about winning a physical battle but also about

Neo finally accepting that he is "The One." His full belief in his own abilities and his purpose is what allows him to triumph in the end, making the victory as much about his internal transformation as it is about defeating the antagonist.

Another important aspect of the Final Challenge is that it often involves sacrifice. In many stories, the hero must give up something significant in order to succeed, whether it's their personal safety, a cherished relationship, or even their life. This sacrifice reinforces the theme of selflessness and highlights the hero's growth from a person focused on their own needs or survival to someone who is willing to put others above themselves. In The Hunger Games, Katniss Everdeen's final challenge is not only to survive the Games but also to protect Peeta and ensure that neither of them is manipulated by the Capitol. Her willingness to sacrifice herself for Peeta's survival demonstrates her commitment to something larger than her own survival.

The Final Challenge is often the most emotionally charged moment in the story because it brings the hero's internal and external conflicts to a resolution. Whether the hero succeeds or fails, the outcome of the Final Challenge defines the hero's legacy and marks the culmination of their journey. This moment offers closure to the story and allows the hero to fully realise their transformation, cementing their role as a hero in the eyes of both the audience and the world they inhabit.

The Final Challenge is the climax of the hero's journey, representing the ultimate test of everything the hero has learned and become. It is a moment of high stakes, deep emotional resonance, and often, sacrifice. The hero's ability to face this challenge successfully is a reflection of their internal growth and transformation, and it ultimately leads to the resolution of the story's central conflict. This stage is what makes the hero's journey meaningful, as it brings the story to its most dramatic and impactful moment.

Chapter Thirteen

Back To Reality, Changed

Summary: The hero returns to their everyday world, but they are transformed by the experience. They bring back something valuable (insight, skills, or rewards) that benefits both them and their community.

Back to Reality, Changed is the final stage in the hero's journey, where the protagonist returns to their ordinary world, but they are no longer the same person. After undergoing trials, challenges, and transformations throughout their adventure, the hero now carries the wisdom, skills, and experiences they gained during their quest. This return marks the conclusion of their journey, but also signals the beginning of a new phase of life—one in which they must integrate the lessons learned into their everyday existence.

In this phase, the hero's changed state is often immediately apparent. Physically, emotionally, or psychologically, they are no longer the person they were when they first set out on their adventure. This transformation is typically the result of the trials they faced during the journey, including internal struggles such as overcoming fear, self-doubt, or personal limitations, as well as external challenges like defeating a villain or solving a problem. Now, as they return to the ordinary world, their new identity is reflected in the way they approach life.

A common theme in the Back to Reality, Changed phase is the hero's sense of alienation or disconnection from the world they left behind. The hero's journey has often been so intense and life-altering that returning to their former routine or environment feels strange or unsatisfying. For example, in The Lord of the Rings, Frodo Baggins returns to the Shire after his long journey to destroy the One Ring, but he finds that he can no longer live the simple life of a hobbit. The scars of his adventure, both physical and emotional, make it difficult for him to fully reintegrate into the life he once knew. This sense of displacement is common in many hero stories, where the hero's transformation sets them apart from their community or former way of life.

However, the hero's return also carries positive aspects. With their newfound knowledge and skills, they are now better equipped to help others or contribute to their community. The hero often brings back something valuable—either literal or metaphorical—that can benefit those around them. This might be a treasure, new knowledge, a skill, or even just a renewed sense of purpose. In The Lion King, Simba returns to Pride Rock after his transformative journey to reclaim his place as king. His experience in exile has changed him, and he brings back not only his courage but also a sense of responsibility to lead and restore balance to his kingdom. The hero's return often signifies hope, renewal, or the beginning of a better future for their community.

The Back to Reality, Changed phase also involves a period of reflection for the hero. This is when they fully realise the impact of their journey on their life and identity. In some stories, this reflection is bittersweet, as the hero acknowledges the sacrifices made and the innocence lost along the way. In other cases, the return is more triumphant, as the hero is celebrated for their achievements and growth. This reflection helps the hero fully understand their transformation and provides closure for both the character and the audience.

An important aspect of this stage is how the hero's personal growth now affects their relationships. Friends, family, and colleagues may view the hero differently, recognising the changes in their character, leadership, or emotional strength. Sometimes, these relationships are strengthened, as the hero's new perspective helps them become a better partner, leader, or friend. In other cases, the hero may feel a sense of separation from those who have not undergone the same transformative experiences, leading to new dynamics in their personal connections.

Back to Reality, Changed is the phase of the hero's journey that highlights the protagonist's return to their ordinary world, forever transformed by their experiences. It reflects the hero's internal growth, their sense of disconnection or renewed purpose, and their ability to bring valuable lessons or resources back to their community. This final stage underscores the ultimate purpose of the hero's journey—not just to achieve personal transformation but to return and make a lasting impact on the world around them.

# Chapter Fourteen

Example Outline - Jack The Soldier

Here's an outline for a story using the 12 steps centred on an ex-army soldier who is pulled back into action after retirement:

1. Everyday Life

- **Character Introduction:** Introduce the protagonist, a retired army soldier named Jack. He now lives a quiet life in a small town, working as a mechanic. Jack enjoys the calm after years of military service, though sometimes he feels restless and disconnected from civilian life.

- **Set the Scene:** Show Jack in his daily routine—fixing cars, visiting his favourite diner, and spending evenings alone in his modest home. He's content but clearly out of place, yearning for something more even if he won't admit it.

2. The Opportunity

- **Inciting Incident:** One day, Jack receives an unexpected visit from an old army buddy, Mike, who brings troubling news. A former military contractor they worked with is involved in illegal arms deals, and some of their old team members have gone missing after investigating.

- **Initial Call to Action:** Mike asks Jack for help in finding the missing team members and stopping the illegal arms deals, but Jack is reluctant, having left that life behind.

3. Doubt and Hesitation

- **Internal Conflict:** Jack wrestles with the decision. He's promised himself he wouldn't get involved in dangerous work again. He's been enjoying his quiet life, and getting involved could threaten the peace he's finally found.

- **External Doubts:** His family and friends advise him to stay out of it, reminding him of the toll his military service took on his mental and physical health. Jack is tempted to ignore Mike's request.

4. Finding a Guide

- **Mentor Introduction:** Jack seeks advice from a former mentor, an old sergeant who now works as a private investigator. The sergeant reminds Jack of his skills, his sense of duty, and the fact that sometimes the world still needs people like him.

- **Guidance and Encouragement:** The sergeant helps Jack realise that turning his back on this could mean more innocent lives are at risk. Jack is encouraged to follow his instincts, even if it's dangerous.

5. Going All In

- **Decision Made:** Jack decides to accept the challenge. He reconnects with old military contacts, dusts off his gear, and starts gathering information on the arms dealer.

- **Preparations Begin:** He agrees to help Mike but sets strict boundaries—this will be a one-time thing, just to help those who are in danger.

6. Challenges and Connections

- **Building the Team:** Jack and Mike begin

tracking down leads and find that more former soldiers are involved, some on the wrong side. Along the way, they recruit allies from their old unit.

- **Obstacles Arise:** They face opposition from corrupt officials, betrayal from people they once trusted, and personal demons as Jack confronts memories from his past service.

- **Strengthening Bonds:** Jack re-establishes strong connections with his old comrades, realising how much he missed this sense of camaraderie.

7. Facing the Big Test

- **Major Confrontation:** Jack and his team track the arms dealer to a hidden base, where a large arms deal is set to go down. They must infiltrate the base and stop the transaction.

- **Life-or-Death Stakes:** The team faces heavily armed mercenaries. Jack must use all of his skills to lead the operation while protecting his team.

8. The Turning Point

- **Unexpected Twist:** During the mission, Jack discovers that one of his closest allies from the military is involved in the arms deal. This betrayal forces Jack to rethink his approach.

- **Internal Shift:** Jack realises that he can't rely on the past and must adapt to the new, morally complex world he's in. He must confront his old friend while staying focused on the mission.

9. The Breakthrough

- **Victory Achieved:** Jack successfully takes down the arms dealer, disarming the situation and saving his team members. He also confronts and arrests his old ally, but not without emotional turmoil.

- **Personal Growth:** In the process, Jack accepts that he can't escape who he is—a protector. He finds a new balance between his military past and civilian life.

10. The Journey Home

- **Return to Civilian Life:** Jack returns to his quiet town, but now with a renewed sense of purpose. He's no longer running from his past but instead embracing his role as someone who can help others.

- **Reflection:** He reflects on how his journey brought him clarity and a deeper understanding of his identity.

11. The Final Challenge

- **Loose Ends:** Just when Jack thinks it's over, he's confronted by one final threat—a corrupt government official who wants to cover up the arms deal.

- **Final Battle:** Jack must outsmart this last antagonist without resorting to violence, using the relationships he's built and the trust he's earned to expose the corruption.

12. Back to Reality, Changed

- **New Life:** Jack returns to his peaceful life, but this time with a sense of fulfilment and acceptance. He continues his work as a mechanic, but now he's more connected to his community, knowing he can make a difference when needed.

- **Changed Man:** He's no longer haunted by his past or struggling with his purpose. Jack has found peace with his dual identity as both a civilian and a protector, ready to step up if the world ever needs him again.

Chapter Fifteen

Example Outline – Emily & Mark

Here's an outline for a story using the 12 steps about a woman whose life is turned upside down when she discovers her fiance is cheating on her with her best friend:

1. Everyday Life

- **Character Introduction:** Introduce the protagonist, Emily, a successful event planner living in a bustling city. She's deeply in love with her fiance, Mark, and they are weeks away from their dream wedding. Everything seems perfect—her career is thriving, and she's excited to start a new chapter in her life.

- **Set the Scene:** Show Emily happily planning the final details of her wedding with her best friend, Sarah, who has been her closest confidante since childhood. They laugh, shop for dresses, and dream about the future, unaware of the storm about to hit.

2. The Opportunity

- **Inciting Incident:** Emily stumbles upon a text on Mark's phone, which hints at a secret relationship. She brushes it off at first, not wanting to believe it, but her curiosity is piqued.

- **Initial Call to Action:** A few days later, she accidentally sees Mark and Sarah together, behaving in a way that makes her worst fears a reality—Mark is cheating on her with her best friend.

3. Doubt and Hesitation

- **Internal Conflict:** Emily is in shock and denial. She doesn't want to believe that the two people she loves most have betrayed her. She contemplates confronting them but is scared of what she might hear.

- **External Pressure:** Her family and friends have no idea what's happening. She struggles with whether to call off the wedding or confront the situation head-on. She feels immense pressure to keep up appearances, especially with the wedding so close.

4. Finding a Guide

- **Mentor Introduction:** Emily confides in an unlikely source—her older sister, a no-nonsense attorney who is always brutally honest. Her sister encourages Emily to face the truth, no matter how painful, and offers practical advice on how to protect herself emotionally and financially.

- **Guidance and Encouragement:** Emily's sister helps her realise that she deserves better, and while it won't be easy, she must confront the betrayal and take control of her life.

5. Going All In

- **Decision Made:** Emily decides to call off the wedding. She confronts Mark and Sarah, and the truth is revealed—they've been seeing each other for months behind her back. Heartbroken, she breaks up with Mark, cuts ties with Sarah, and moves out of the apartment she shared with Mark.

- **New Life Begins:** Emily moves into a small, temporary apartment, determined to rebuild her life from scratch. She's scared, vulnerable, and unsure of what her future holds, but she knows she has to move forward.

6. Challenges and Connections

- **Personal Challenges:** Emily struggles with the loneliness and heartbreak of losing not only her fiance but also her best friend. She questions her self-worth and feels lost in a world that no longer makes sense.

- **New Connections:** In the midst of this turmoil, Emily reconnects with old friends she'd drifted apart from during her relationship with Mark. She also starts therapy to work through her emotions and begins focusing on self-care.

- **Facing Society:** Emily feels the pressure of societal judgment. Her family and friends, some of whom don't know the full story, ask why the wedding is cancelled. She has to navigate the painful process of explaining the betrayal.

7. Facing the Big Test

- **Confronting Her Pain:** Emily is invited to a wedding—a mutual friend's—with both Mark and Sarah attending. She has to decide whether to go and face them, or hide away and continue avoiding the pain.

- **Emotional Battle:** Emily ultimately chooses to attend, not for them, but for herself. She confronts the situation head-on, refusing to be defined by their betrayal, and presents herself confidently at the wedding, even though it hurts to see them together.

8. The Turning Point

- **Moment of Clarity:** At the wedding, Emily has a breakthrough when she realises that her identity and happiness do not depend on Mark or Sarah. She sees their relationship for what it is—built on deceit—and understands that she is better off without them.

- **Internal Shift:** Emily chooses to let go of her anger and decides to focus on her own future. She realises that this chapter of her life, while painful, is also an opportunity for her to start fresh.

9. The Breakthrough

- **Personal Victory:** Emily begins to thrive. She throws herself into her career, landing a huge event planning contract that pushes her business to new heights. She starts a new hobby, takes up yoga, and begins dating again—slowly, on her own terms.

- **Emotional Growth:** She no longer feels defined by her past relationship or the betrayal. Emily's confidence returns, and she feels more empowered than ever.

10. The Journey Home

- **Returning to Her New Normal:** Emily moves into a new, beautiful apartment that represents her fresh start. She has fully embraced her independence and created a life that reflects who she is now, rather than the person she was before.

- **Reflection:** She takes time to reflect on her journey, realising that while she was heartbroken, she has come out stronger and more self-aware than ever.

11. The Final Challenge

- **Unexpected Encounter:** Mark reaches out, asking to meet. He tells her that things with Sarah didn't work out and he wants her back. This is Emily's final test—whether to let her past pull her back or stand firm in her new life.

- **Final Decision:** Emily meets with Mark but tells him that she has moved on and no longer needs him in her life. She leaves the meeting with closure, knowing that she made the right decision to let go.

12. Back to Reality, Changed

- **New Life, New Mindset:** Emily is back in her life, but she's a completely transformed person. She's confident, happy, and independent. She knows she's capable of facing life's challenges on her own terms.

- **Changed Woman:** She's no longer the woman who was reliant on her relationship or her best friend for validation. Emily is now the hero of her own story, focused on building a life full of love, friendship, and personal fulfilment on her own terms.

Chapter Sixteen

Example Outline - Max The Dog

Here's an outline for a story using the 12 steps, centred on an animal living in a zoo who is taken home by a cruel boy and later rescued, finding love and happiness in a new home:

1. Everyday Life

- **Character Introduction:** Introduce the protagonist, Max, a playful and curious dog who lives in the zoo's petting area. Max is beloved by the zoo staff and enjoys interacting with visitors, especially children who come to pet him. Life at the zoo is simple, but Max feels content and safe in this familiar environment.

- **Set the Scene:** Show Max's daily routine in the zoo—playing with other animals, basking in the sun, and being well cared for by the zookeepers who feed and groom him.

2. The Opportunity

- **Inciting Incident:** One day, a boy named Kyle visits the zoo with his parents. Kyle seems intrigued by Max, but his intentions are not kind. After much convincing, Kyle's wealthy parents decide to adopt Max and take him home, thinking it will teach their son responsibility.

- **Initial Call to Action:** Max is taken away from his familiar surroundings at the zoo and is excited at first, thinking this could be a new adventure. However, something feels off about the boy's behaviour.

3. Doubt and Hesitation

- **Internal Conflict:** Max arrives at Kyle's home and quickly realises that it's not a loving environment. Kyle is cruel, pulling at Max's ears, teasing him, and locking him in a small, dark room when no one is around. Max begins to doubt whether this new life is something he can survive.

- **External Challenges:** Max misses the zoo and the gentle care of the zookeepers. He feels confused, scared, and unsure of what to do. He tries to please Kyle but is met with more cruelty.

4. Finding a Guide

- **Mentor Introduction:** While trapped in Kyle's house, Max meets a stray cat, Luna, who sneaks in through a window. Luna tells Max about the outside world, where there are kind people and animals who live freely. She encourages Max not to give up and shares survival tips on how to cope with Kyle's cruelty until an opportunity for escape arises.

- **Guidance and Encouragement:** Luna helps Max understand that he deserves better and gives him hope that there are better homes out there. She becomes a source of emotional support during Max's darkest days.

5. Going All In

- **Decision Made:** Max decides he can no longer just endure Kyle's torment. He starts to act smarter, staying out of Kyle's way and conserving his energy for when an opportunity for escape arises.

- **Survival Instincts Kick In:** Max begins to listen to Luna's advice and becomes more resourceful, learning how to hide from Kyle when necessary and how to make the most of the little food and comfort he gets.

6. Challenges and Connections

- **Personal Challenges:** Max faces daily torment from Kyle, who grows more aggressive, sometimes throwing objects at Max and yelling at him for no reason. Max's spirit is battered, but he holds on to hope.

- **New Connections:** Max finds comfort in the other animals in the neighbourhood, especially Luna, who checks on him regularly. Together, they devise small plans to help Max cope with the isolation and cruelty.

- **Physical Struggles:** Max begins to lose weight and energy as Kyle's neglect worsens, and he realises he needs help soon or he may not survive.

7. Facing the Big Test

- **Major Confrontation:** One night, Kyle goes too far and injures Max badly during one of his outbursts. Max is at his lowest point, physically weakened and emotionally shattered. He's unsure if he can survive another day in Kyle's home.

- **Life-or-Death Stakes:** Max's survival is in question. His only hope is that someone will see his plight and rescue him before it's too late.

8. The Turning Point

- **Unexpected Rescue:** One day, a neighbour hears the commotion and sees Max's terrible condition. This kind neighbour contacts an animal rescue service, reporting the abuse and neglect.

- **Internal Shift:** Max realises that there are people who care and want to help him. For the first time in a long time, he feels a spark of hope.

9. The Breakthrough

- **Rescue Arrives:** The animal rescue team arrives and takes Max away from Kyle's home. Max is weak but relieved to be free from the cruelty. He's taken to a shelter where he's given medical care, food, and love for the first time in what feels like forever.

- **Emotional Growth:** Max's faith in humans is slowly restored as the shelter staff show him kindness and affection. He begins to heal, both physically and emotionally.

10. The Journey Home

- **Healing Process:** Max starts to recover at

the shelter, slowly regaining his strength and trust in people. The shelter becomes a safe space for him, and he meets other animals who have been through similar experiences.

- **Reflection:** Max reflects on his journey and realises that despite the trauma he endured, he has survived and grown stronger. He's grateful for the kindness of strangers who gave him a second chance.

11. The Final Challenge

- **New Adoption:** After several weeks, a kind family visits the shelter and expresses interest in adopting Max. He's hesitant at first, unsure if he can trust people again. This is Max's final test—whether to open his heart to love again or remain closed off in fear.

- **Final Decision:** Max decides to take a leap of faith and trust the new family. He goes home with them, determined to start over and embrace a life of love and safety.

12. Back to Reality, Changed

- **New Life, New Home:** Max thrives in his new home, where he's treated with care and affection. He now lives in a peaceful, loving environment with a family that adores him. He plays in the yard, enjoys long walks, and sleeps in a cosy bed each night.

- **Changed Dog:** Max is no longer the frightened, abused dog he once was. He has found his strength, survived adversity, and is now flourishing in a life where he is cherished. Max has been transformed by his journey, not just surviving but truly thriving in his new, happy reality.

Chapter Seventeen

Example Outline - Emma & Ted

Here's an outline for a thriller story using the 12 steps about Emma, a woman who falls in love with a seemingly perfect law student named Ted, only to discover that he is a serial killer, and she must find a way to escape before it's too late:

1. Everyday Life

- **Character Introduction:** Emma, a kind-hearted and intelligent young woman, is a college senior studying psychology. She's well-liked, has a close-knit group of friends, and is generally optimistic about life. Emma dreams of a career in counselling and enjoys her peaceful, structured life.

- **Set the Scene:** Emma meets Ted, a charming and handsome law student, at a campus party. Ted is the picture of the perfect boyfriend—polite, ambitious, and thoughtful. They begin dating, and everything seems wonderful. Ted showers her with attention, and Emma falls deeply in love with him.

2. The Opportunity

- **Inciting Incident:** Ted and Emma's relationship progresses quickly. Ted invites Emma to stay with him at his off-campus apartment. She's excited, believing their relationship is growing more serious. At first, everything seems perfect—Ted is loving and attentive, and Emma feels like she's found "the one."

- **The Start of Suspicion:** However, Emma starts to notice small oddities about Ted's behaviour. He becomes distant, sometimes disappearing without explanation for long periods. She brushes off her initial concerns, thinking he's just busy with law school.

3. Doubt and Hesitation

- **Internal Conflict:** Emma starts to feel uneasy. Ted's mood changes frequently, and he starts becoming secretive about his whereabouts. He's not the attentive, loving man she first met. She begins to wonder if she's imagining things or if something is really wrong.

- **Red Flags:** Emma finds strange items in Ted's apartment—like women's jewellery that doesn't belong to her—and odd scratches on his arms. When she asks him about them, he dodges her questions with charming excuses. Emma is torn between confronting

Ted and ignoring her instincts, as she still deeply cares for him.

4. Finding a Guide

- **Mentor Introduction:** Emma confides in her best friend, Megan, who encourages her to trust her gut. Megan does some research and finds unsettling news articles about women who have gone missing near campus. She urges Emma to be careful and to investigate further, but Emma is still hesitant to believe Ted could be involved in anything dangerous.

- **Guidance and Encouragement:** Megan pushes Emma to dig deeper and protect herself. She tells Emma to watch for more warning signs and suggests finding a way to gather evidence before confronting Ted.

5. Going All In

- **Decision Made:** After weeks of growing suspicion, Emma decides she needs to know the truth. She discreetly starts going through Ted's things when he's not home, looking for anything that could explain his behaviour.

- **Horrifying Discovery:** Emma finds disturbing evidence—a hidden stash of photographs of missing women, items belonging to them, and articles about unsolved murders. Everything points to Ted being involved in these women's disappearances.

6. Challenges and Connections

- **Escalating Danger:** Emma is terrified but knows she needs to escape. Ted becomes more erratic and controlling, sensing that Emma is pulling away. He starts questioning her every move, becoming possessive and showing signs of violent tendencies.

- **Isolation:** Emma feels trapped, as Ted rarely

leaves her alone anymore. She tries to reach out to Megan, but Ted becomes suspicious of her phone calls and texts, making it difficult for Emma to contact anyone for help.

- **Staying Smart:** Emma must keep her fear hidden and pretend everything is fine while secretly planning her escape.

7. Facing the Big Test

- **Ted's True Nature Revealed:** One night, Ted's dark side fully emerges. He becomes aggressive and threatening, hinting that he knows Emma has found out his secret. He confronts her, his charm gone, replaced by cold, calculating malice. Emma realises her life is in immediate danger.

- **Life-or-Death Stakes:** Ted implies that he's done this before, and now that Emma knows too much, she's next. Emma has to act quickly, or she won't survive the night.

8. The Turning Point

- **Emma's Decision to Fight Back:** Realising that she has no other option, Emma decides she must escape by any means necessary. She stops playing the role of the frightened girlfriend and instead begins thinking like a survivor.

- **Internal Shift:** Emma's fear turns to determination. She won't let Ted control her fate. She remembers Megan's advice about staying calm and finding an opportunity to flee.

9. The Breakthrough

- **Escape Plan:** Emma manages to send a coded message to Megan through a photo on social media, alerting her that she's in danger. Megan immediately contacts the police, but Emma knows they might not arrive in time.

- **Moment of Action:** While Ted is distracted, Emma uses her knowledge of psychology to manipulate him, pretending to trust him again. She waits for the right moment, then uses his own apartment's layout against him, locking him in a room and making a run for it.

10. The Journey Home

- **Fleeing for Her Life:** Emma runs through the night, evading Ted as he breaks out and chases after her. She manages to find a nearby neighbour's house and bangs on the door, begging for help. The police, alerted by Megan, arrive just in time.

- **Reflection:** As Ted is arrested, Emma realises how close she came to losing her life. She's shaken but grateful to have survived. However, she knows the emotional scars of this ordeal will stay with her for a long time.

11. The Final Challenge

- **Dealing with the Aftermath:** Even after Ted is behind bars, Emma struggles with the trauma of what happened. She can't shake the feeling that he could somehow return, and she's haunted by nightmares. She feels unsafe and paranoid, questioning her judgment and trust in others.

- **Rebuilding Her Life:** With the support of Megan and therapy, Emma begins to heal. She realises that surviving isn't just about physically escaping—it's about mentally and emotionally reclaiming her life.

12. Back to Reality, Changed

- **New Life, New Strength:** Emma is no longer the naïve, trusting woman she was before. She is stronger, more self-aware, and determined not to let the trauma define her.

She changes her major to criminal psychology, hoping to one day help others who have experienced similar trauma.

- **Changed Woman:** Emma is transformed by her experience, but instead of being defined by fear, she channels her pain into purpose. She continues with her studies, focused on moving forward, knowing she narrowly escaped the most dangerous chapter of her life.

Chapter Eighteen

Example Outline - Mike & Sarah (comedy)

Here's an outline for a comedy story using the 12 steps, centred on Mike, an awkward guy who's been secretly in love with Sarah for years, but she's about to marry his best friend Jason, a charming womaniser:

1. Everyday Life

- **Character Introduction:** Mike is a socially awkward, nerdy guy in his early 30s who lives alone in a small apartment. He spends most of his time playing video games, talking to his pet fish, and overthinking every social interaction. He's not great with people and often says the wrong thing at the worst times.

- **Set the Scene:** Mike has been in love with Sarah, his co-worker, for years. The problem? She's dating Jason—Mike's best friend since college. Jason is a smooth-talking, good-looking womaniser who seems to have it all, and Mike feels invisible in comparison.

2. The Opportunity

- **Inciting Incident:** Sarah announces that she's getting married to Jason. The news is a crushing blow to Mike, who's secretly been holding out hope that one day she'd notice him. To make matters worse, Jason asks Mike to be his best man.

- **Initial Call to Action:** Mike wants to stop the wedding but has no idea how. He's too awkward to express his feelings and knows no one would take him seriously if he did.

3. Doubt and Hesitation

- **Internal Conflict:** Mike spends days agonising over what to do. Should he just let Sarah marry Jason? After all, she seems happy, right? But Mike knows Jason's secret—Jason is a notorious cheat and has already been unfaithful multiple times. Mike feels a moral obligation to save Sarah, but he's terrified of ruining their friendship or making things worse.

- **Social Awkwardness:** Mike tries to rehearse telling Sarah the truth but keeps fumbling his words. His attempts to practice confessing his love to his bathroom mirror are awkward and uncomfortable.

4. Finding a Guide

- **Mentor Introduction:** Mike seeks advice from his eccentric, conspiracy-theorist neighbour, Mrs. Jenkins. She's the type who wears tinfoil hats and thinks the government is watching, but she's oddly perceptive about relationships. She tells Mike that the universe has given him a sign, and it's up to him to stop the wedding and win the girl.

- **Guidance and Encouragement:** Mrs. Jenkins suggests a completely bonkers plan involving skywriting and public declarations, but Mike settles on a simpler plan—he'll show Sarah who Jason really is by catching him in the act.

5. Going All In

- **Decision Made:** Determined, Mike decides to go all in. He starts secretly following Jason, convinced that if he can catch Jason cheating, he'll be able to save Sarah from a lifetime of misery. Of course, Mike is terrible at stealth, and his attempts to tail Jason lead to a series of misadventures—tripping over trash cans, falling out of bushes, and almost getting caught multiple times.

- **The Plan:** Mike manages to snap some incriminating photos of Jason with another woman, but of course, they're blurry and look more like Bigfoot sightings than real evidence.

6. Challenges and Connections

- **Obstacles Arise:** Just when Mike thinks he has enough evidence, his phone falls into a fountain, ruining the photos. Frustrated, he tries to tell Sarah directly, but she's busy with wedding preparations and brushes him off. Meanwhile, Jason remains as smooth and unbothered as ever.

- **Failed Attempts:** Mike awkwardly tries to

warn Sarah during a wedding cake tasting by knocking the cake over, making it look like he's jealous rather than trying to help. Each attempt to stop the wedding goes wrong.

- **New Allies:** Mike accidentally reveals his crush to Sarah's quirky bridesmaid, Lisa, who agrees to help him. Lisa is sharp and quick-witted and suggests a more foolproof plan to catch Jason in the act.

7. Facing the Big Test

- **Major Confrontation:** Mike and Lisa set a trap for Jason by luring him to a fake "bachelor party" that they've arranged at a bar. Their goal is to expose him in front of Sarah. Things go wrong when the fake bachelor party spirals into chaos, with Mike getting stuck in an awkward karaoke performance and Jason slipping away.

- **Life-or-Death (Socially) Stakes:** With the

wedding just days away, Mike knows he has one last chance to stop it. Feeling defeated, he contemplates giving up.

8. The Turning Point

- **Moment of Clarity:** At the rehearsal dinner, Mike overhears Jason bragging to his friends about how he can't wait to "have fun" even after he's married. It's the final straw for Mike. He realises he can't just stand by and let Sarah marry a guy who doesn't respect her.

- **Internal Shift:** Mike finally finds his courage. This is no longer about getting the girl—it's about doing the right thing. He knows he needs to tell Sarah the truth, no matter how awkward or uncomfortable it is.

9. The Breakthrough

- **Confession Time:** During the wedding rehearsal, Mike interrupts and blurts out everything in front of everyone—his feelings for Sarah, Jason's cheating, and how he's been a coward for not speaking up sooner. It's an awkward, rambling speech, but it's heartfelt.

- **The Reveal:** Just as Sarah starts to doubt Mike's words, Jason's phone buzzes—another girl texting him. Sarah checks it, and the truth finally comes out. Jason's smug façade crumbles.

10. The Journey Home

- **Aftermath:** The wedding is called off, and Jason storms out in disgrace. Sarah, shocked and heartbroken, turns to Mike, not knowing how to process everything. Mike, though awkward, tries to comfort her, but mostly just offers her a really weird hug and a cup of tea.

- **Reflection:** Sarah thanks Mike for his honesty, even though she's still processing the betrayal. Mike, though awkward, realises he's done the right thing and feels a strange sense of pride.

11. The Final Challenge

- **Decision Time for Sarah:** After a few days, Sarah asks Mike to meet her for coffee. Mike assumes she's going to tell him she's moving on, but instead, she tells him that she's reevaluating her life and the people she surrounds herself with. She admits she always admired Mike's kindness but didn't see him that way—until now.

- **Mike's Own Struggles:** Mike's final test isn't about winning Sarah's heart—it's about staying true to who he is. He awkwardly stumbles over his words, but ultimately tells her that whatever happens, he's just happy he could help her.

12. Back to Reality, Changed

- **New Beginning:** Mike doesn't get the girl right away, but Sarah and he begin spending more time together, this time as genuine friends. Slowly, their friendship grows into something deeper, and Mike finally feels comfortable in his own skin.

- **Changed Man:** Mike isn't the bumbling, invisible guy he once was. He's more confident, and while he's still awkward, he's learned that it's okay to be himself. He's proven to himself (and Sarah) that sometimes the nice guy really can make a difference, even if it doesn't go perfectly.

Chapter Nineteen

Example Outline – Mark & Emma

Here's an outline for a thriller story using the 12 steps, centred on Mark, an ex-SAS soldier, and his best friend Brian's daughter, Emma, who is kidnapped by a human trafficking gang. Mark initially resists getting involved, but after Brian's death, he is driven to take down the gang and save Emma.

1. Everyday Life

- **Character Introduction:** Introduce Emma, a bright and independent 19-year-old college student. She's recently started working part-time at a local bar to earn extra money, enjoying a sense of newfound freedom. Meanwhile, Mark, her next-door neighbour, is a retired SAS soldier. He lives a quiet, solitary life, doing odd jobs around town and trying to leave his military past behind. He and Emma are close—she looks up to him as a protective uncle figure.

- **Set the Scene:** Show the close-knit relationship between Mark, Brian (Emma's father), and Emma. They have Sunday barbecues, and there's a strong sense of community. Mark is a man of few words but has a soft spot for Emma.

2. The Opportunity

- **Inciting Incident:** Emma doesn't come home after a night working at the bar. Brian starts to worry when she doesn't answer her phone, and after a day of silence, he begins to panic. Brian discovers that the bar Emma works at is connected to a dangerous trafficking ring and believes something sinister has happened to her.

- **Call for Help:** Brian asks Mark to help him investigate. At first, Mark is reluctant, not wanting to get involved with something that could bring violence back into his life. He advises Brian to let the police handle it.

3. Doubt and Hesitation

- **Internal Conflict:** Mark struggles with the decision to help. He has spent years trying to escape the violence of his past, and getting involved could pull him back into that dark world. But he feels a strong sense of responsibility to Emma and Brian, who are like family to him.

- **External Pressure:** Brian is desperate and determined to confront the traffickers himself if Mark won't help. Mark warns him it's too dangerous, but Brian won't listen. Mark reluctantly agrees to come along, thinking he can at least ensure Brian doesn't get hurt.

4. Finding a Guide

- **Mentor Introduction:** Mark reaches out to an old military contact, an intelligence officer who provides him with information on the bar and the gang that runs it. His contact warns him that the traffickers are ruthless and dangerous, but offers some advice on how to approach them.

- **Guidance and Encouragement:** Mark's contact subtly reminds him that he still has the skills to handle this situation, even though he's been out of action for years. Mark starts to realise that he may be the only one capable of getting Emma back.

5. Going All In

- **Decision Made:** Mark and Brian head to the bar where Emma was last seen. Mark intends to keep things under control and talk their way in, but Brian, driven by panic and fury, confronts the traffickers too aggressively.

- **Things Go Wrong:** The situation escalates. The traffickers react violently, and Mark quickly realises that Emma has been taken by the gang, but they won't reveal where. A fight breaks out, and Mark manages to get them out alive, but Brian is injured.

6. Challenges and Connections

- **Personal Challenges:** With Brian severely injured, Mark takes him to safety. Brian is determined to continue the search for his daughter, despite his injuries, but Mark insists on taking over. Mark knows the gang will stop at nothing to cover their tracks, and they're now aware that he's looking for Emma.

- **Emotional Strain:** Emma's absence weighs heavily on Mark as he begins tracking down leads on his own. He feels responsible for Brian and Emma, and guilt creeps in—if he had acted sooner, maybe they wouldn't be in this mess.

- **New Allies:** Mark reconnects with some of his old SAS comrades, who reluctantly agree to help him. They provide him with tactical support, weapons, and additional intel on the trafficking ring.

7. Facing the Big Test

- **Major Confrontation:** Mark and Brian trace Emma's whereabouts to a remote warehouse owned by the trafficking gang. Desperate to save her, Brian charges in before Mark can stop him. During the ensuing shootout,

Brian is killed, leaving Mark devastated and angry.

- **Life-or-Death Stakes:** Mark is now alone, and with Brian's death, he feels personally responsible for saving Emma. He knows this is his last chance to bring her home alive.

8. The Turning Point

- **Moment of Clarity:** After Brian's death, Mark's resolve hardens. He realises that he can no longer keep running from his past. His skills as a soldier are the only thing that will save Emma, and he must use everything he knows to bring her back. Mark sets aside his personal demons and fully commits to the mission.

- **Internal Shift:** Mark stops holding back. He's no longer just helping Brian—he's doing this for Emma and for himself, to make up for all the times he hesitated.

9. The Breakthrough

- **Rescue Mission:** Mark infiltrates the gang's hideout alone, using all of his military training. He quietly takes down the guards, navigating through the facility with precision and stealth. In the final room, he finds Emma, terrified but alive, locked in a holding cell.

- **Emotional Growth:** Mark frees Emma, and the two share an emotional moment. Emma, shaken and traumatised, clings to Mark, but he reassures her that she's safe now. Mark, who has always been emotionally distant, feels a surge of protectiveness and relief.

10. The Journey Home

- **Escape and Aftermath:** Mark and Emma escape the hideout, with the traffickers in pursuit. After a tense chase and final confrontation, Mark eliminates the last of the gang members, ensuring they can no longer hurt anyone.

- **Reflection:** As they make their way back home, Mark reflects on the cost of the mission. He has lost his best friend, but he's saved Emma. He's come to terms with the violence of his past, realising that sometimes, it's necessary to protect those you love.

11. The Final Challenge

- **Helping Emma Heal:** The final challenge isn't just about saving Emma physically—it's about helping her heal emotionally. Mark realises that rescuing her from the traffickers was just the beginning. Emma is traumatised, and Mark feels responsible for helping her rebuild her life.

- **Mark's Own Struggles:** Mark also faces his own internal struggles. He's haunted by the death of Brian and questions whether he could have done more. But he knows he must stay strong for Emma.

12. Back to Reality, Changed

- **New Life for Emma:** Emma, while still recovering, begins to rebuild her life. She's stronger now, no longer the carefree girl she once was, but she's determined to move forward. She knows Mark saved her life, and their bond deepens as they lean on each other for support.

- **Changed Man:** Mark returns to his quiet life, but he's no longer trying to escape his past. He's reconnected with his purpose and understands that his skills are meant to protect and save others. He's at peace with who he is now, having faced his demons and come out on the other side.

- **Moving Forward:** Mark stays close to Emma, helping her through her recovery.

The two form an even stronger bond, not just as protector and protected, but as survivors who faced unimaginable darkness and emerged stronger.

Chapter Twenty

Final Chapter: A Practical Tool for Writers

As you've seen throughout this book, it's designed to be just that: practical. It's not a deep exploration of storytelling theory or a guide that covers every tiny detail about how to write the perfect story. If that's what you're after, I'd strongly recommend reading *The Writer's Journey* or *The Hero with a Thousand Faces*. There are plenty of other books out there—hundreds of pages long—that go into intricate detail about story structure.

But this book? This is for writers who want to *get writing*.

It's for those of us who need something simple and functional, a tool that helps us organise our ideas and get straight into the writing process. The 12 steps in this book provide a straightforward framework to build your story—no frills, no distractions. From the very first page, you have everything you need to outline your story quickly. You can refer to the 12 steps, check the relevant chapters for more context, and get your outline together in no time.

This book isn't about percentages or rigid structures. I don't bother with things like "the first act should be 10% of the story," or "this turning point should happen at exactly 25%." That's not my style. I prefer to write based on what feels right for the story. This book gives you the freedom to do the same. You can use the 12 steps loosely, or stick to them more closely if that suits your approach—it's entirely up to you.

I wrote this for myself, as a practical tool I can pull out whenever I need to. Whether I'm working on a sales presentation, a webinar, a novel, or a short story, I know I can rely on these 12 steps to get the structure right. It's small and portable, designed to fit in my bag so I can take it anywhere. When inspiration strikes, I've got a simple guide to keep me on track.

If you're a writer who regularly produces content—whether it's fiction, non-fiction, or even copywriting—this book can help you stay organised and focused. It's not about being perfect; it's about making sure your ideas flow and your story is coherent, using a reliable framework to guide you.

I hope you find this book as helpful as I do. If it sparks some ideas or helps you write more efficiently, then it's done its job. This isn't a strict rulebook—it's a flexible tool to make your writing process smoother, whether you're working on a novel, a screenplay, or anything in between.

Thanks for reading, and I hope it serves you well. If you'd like to check out my other books, you'll find them in the next chapter.

Cheers, and happy writing!
Mike Martin

Chapter Twenty-One

More Books by Mike Martin

More Books by Mike Martin
As we reach the conclusion of this book, it's the perfect time to introduce you to more resources that will expand your understanding of marketing, sales, and entrepreneurship. Each of my books is designed to provide clear, actionable insights that you can apply immediately. Let's take a brief look at each one:

In A World Full of Sheep, Fuck You I'm an Entrepreneur *(the best book I ever wrote)*

For those who dare to break the mould and forge their own path, this book is a manifesto for entrepreneurial rebellion. It's about rejecting conformity, embracing individuality, and pushing boundaries in business and life. I share personal stories, practical advice, and the mindset shifts needed to thrive in a world that often values the status quo. This book is for the true mavericks who are ready to say, "I'm an entrepreneur, and I'm unapologetically proud of it."

The Sales Parables

This book uses storytelling to teach valuable lessons in sales. Through engaging stories and real-world examples, I provide insights into clever sales strategies and techniques that stick. It's designed to inspire and educate, showing you how to connect with customers and close deals effectively. If you've ever struggled with sales or want to refine your approach, *The Sales Parables* offers timeless wisdom in an engaging format.

The One Sentence Marketing Course

In this book, I distil everything you need to know about marketing into a single, powerful sentence. It's a no-nonsense guide that breaks down marketing to its core principles, giving you a straightforward formula to apply to any industry or business. If you want to cut through the noise and master marketing with clarity, this book is your go-to guide.

The One Sentence Storytelling Course

This book teaches you the art of storytelling in its simplest form. I break down storytelling into a single sentence structure that you can use to craft compelling narratives for marketing, sales, and communication. Whether you want to captivate an audience, close a deal, or simply engage people better, this book provides you with a practical framework to become a powerful storyteller.

How to Create The Perfect Sales Webinar

Webinars are one of the most powerful tools in digital marketing, and this book shows you exactly how to craft the perfect one. From structuring your message to engaging your audience and closing sales, this book covers every detail you need to know. Whether you're new to webinars or looking to refine your strategy, you'll find all the essential techniques for turning your presentations into high-converting sales machines.

Get Rich With Digital Real Estate

This book explores the lucrative world of digital real estate. Learn how to build and profit from online properties, dominate local markets, and create streams of passive income. It's a practical guide for entrepreneurs looking to leverage digital assets for long-term wealth. If you're interested in building an online empire, this book provides the blueprint to make it happen.

Each of these books is crafted to empower you with the skills, knowledge, and mindset needed to excel in business and beyond. If you've found value in this book, you'll undoubtedly discover even more tools and inspiration in these titles. Explore, learn, and take your entrepreneurial journey to the next level with my collection of practical and insightful resources.

I'm also available to speak on these subjects for podcasts, events, and other platforms. To schedule a conversation, simply book a chat with me at mikemartin.uk.

All the best,
Mike Martin
https://mikemartin.uk

Made in the USA
Middletown, DE
07 June 2025